INCREDIBLY

by Alain Cirou

**Series director :
François Cherrier**

FAR

new Discovery
BOOKS
New York

Eyes in the night

Modern astronomers no longer gaze directly at the sky. They operate computer keyboards and telescopes, enormous glass giants that capture the movements of the stars. When a star is visible on the monitor, the camera starts to photograph. The process takes many hours, during which the immense funnel collects tiny specks of light that come from the outer reaches of space. This light is then directed at a photographic plate in a photon counter. Electronic detectors have replaced the unaided eye and have tremendously improved image quality and telescopic capacity. Astronomers now travel to deserted mountaintops in search of pure skies unpolluted by human activity. There the atmosphere is dry, stable, and free of "turbulence." Once all these conditions have been met, observations can begin.

The sky offers a grandiose sight to the naked eye. Few know how to fully appreciate it, although it is easy: the only criteria for observing the stars is a healthy curiosity. Imagination is perhaps a necessary counterpart; without it, the unthinkable is hard to accept: these thousands of visible stars, similar to our sun, represent an insignificant quantity in the immensity of the universe. In fact, an infinite number of stars exists. Scientists even say that there are more stars in the universe than there are grains of sand on the earth. This disconcerting fact presents a perplexing challenge: A major part of the universe is invisible to us, and as far as our instruments can reach, a myriad of stars and an infinity of galaxies continue to appear.

Hawaii is home to one of astronomy's most important observatories. Every night, the 12-foot Franco-Canadian telescope at the summit of Mauna Kea is aimed at the stars.

The La Silla observatory in the Chilean Andes is one of the largest in the world. Astronomers have found a meteorological Eldorado south of the Atacama desert. The dome of the observatory opens as soon as night falls. Six hundred astronomers from all over the world come here every year to observe stars, galaxies, and distant quasars. Telescopes do not, in fact, enlarge stars. They function rather as gigantic light funnels. The larger the glass mirror, the larger the light-gathering surface. Light photons from a distant galaxy strike the reflecting surface and are then focused onto sensitive cameras. The more photons that are gathered, the brighter the image of the galaxy, allowing scientists to pursue their explorations to ever greater distances.

Planets in the sky

They look like brilliant stars and move at their own speed through the constellations. Long ago, Greek astronomers called them "planets," which means "wanderers," because their celestial paths disturbed the tranquility of the star-filled vault. They are all famous. The Evening Star is the first to shine in the evening and the last to disappear in the morning: the most luminous body after the Sun and the Moon is the planet Venus. The largest? Surrounded by bands of clouds, with a large red eye, the planet that brought Galileo before the Inquisition when he postulated that Earth was not the center of the universe: Jupiter. The most beautiful? The jewel of the solar system, like a gold ring that encircles a pearl on black velvet: Saturn, of course. There are nine planets, and we live on the most hospitable of them all. All lie at astronomical distances from Earth. Light travels to the Moon in one second, while it takes one and a half hours to reach Saturn! Imagine then the fabulous voyages of the space probes, which bear legendary names such as Pioneer, Viking, or Voyager, modern-day sailing ships launched to discover new worlds.

To the naked eye, Mars appears to be no more than a red dot in the sky. This planet, which lies between Earth and Jupiter, was dedicated to the god of war, first by the Greeks and later by the Romans because of its bloodlike color. Who could then have suspected the existence of volcanoes, deserts, dry riverbeds, and polar caps?

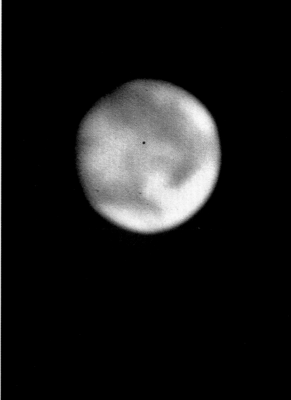

This is undoubtedly one of the best images of Mars taken by astronomers observing the planet with an astronomical telescope. Mars is about half the size of Earth. The spots visible on the surface of the planet are difficult to interpret. We now know that vast dust storms can obscure the planet's surface for several days. We also know that there are no traces of civilization on the surface (even ancient ones).

These celestial globes are no longer merely lights suspended among the stars; we now know they consist of deserts, mountains, volcanoes, and boulders of ice.

Mars, the red planet. In 1976 the American space probe Viking discovered the most Earthlike planet in the solar system. Three gigantic extinct volcanoes loom over the large lava deserts. A deep fracture in the Martian crust, Vallis Marineris, extends for more than 300 miles and includes a system of channels up to 20,000 feet deep. This surface reflects the tumultuous past of the red planet. Researchers in the future have many mysteries to unravel. Was life able to develop on Mars? Why did the water dry up? How did the atmosphere become so thin, and, above all, why didn't this planet develop in the same way as Earth?

VENUS: AN INFERNO UNDER THE CLOUDS

Venus, an enchantingly bright planet, so close to Earth and yet so hostile to man and his numerous attempts to explore it. A globe the size of our planet surrounded by a cloak of clouds and close enough to the Sun to be scorched by its heat. A small detail: the atmosphere is so dense that the surface is perpetually shrouded. And what a surface! In the 1950s an amateur French astronomer, Charles Boyer, discovered that the atmosphere revolved around Venus in four days. He didn't know, however, that it travels 60 times faster than the planet itself. Another surprise: the planet, like the atmosphere, rotates in the opposite direction from all the other planets! Under these clouds, the ground is drier than the most arid desert on Earth and, at 878° F, hot enough to melt zinc. Even if an astronaut could survive such extreme temperatures, he would have to withstand rains of sulfuric acid and a pressure equal to that at 3,280 feet below sea level. How could a planet that lies so close to us have been transformed into such an inferno? Some twenty missions have been launched to study Venus. The most recent one, Magellan, was equipped with radars that were able to pierce through the cloud layer. The landscapes it discovered revealed an entirely unknown and complex world, dominated by astonishing volcanic structures that jut up along the horizon, creating sharp-edged landscapes.

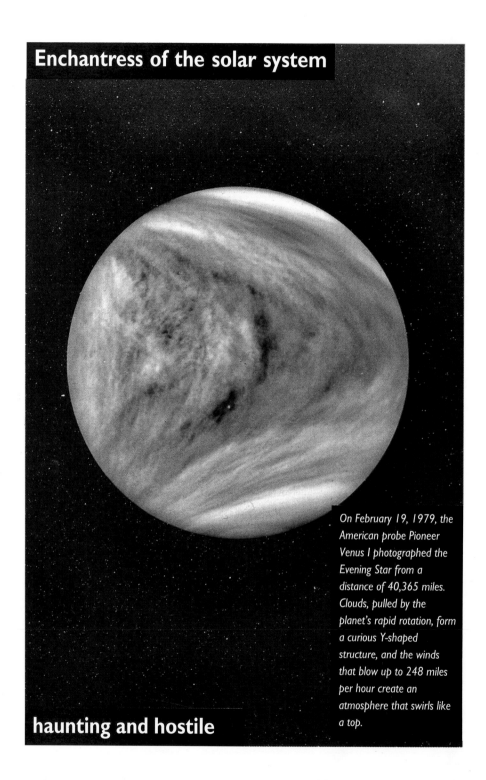

Enchantress of the solar system

haunting and hostile

On February 19, 1979, the American probe Pioneer Venus I photographed the Evening Star from a distance of 40,365 miles. Clouds, pulled by the planet's rapid rotation, form a curious Y-shaped structure, and the winds that blow up to 248 miles per hour create an atmosphere that swirls like a top.

The evolution of Earth's neighbor has long intrigued astronomers: How could a planet so close to our world transform itself into something so different? To understand this about twenty space missions have been made to study Venus.

This is one of the most expensive images obtained by space exploration—also one of the most precious. To obtain it, the Soviets sent 18 vessels, veritable monsters encased in steel plates and insulated to withstand the extreme temperatures and pressures. An analysis of the soil samples conducted automatically by the Venera probe confirmed that these large rocky plates were formed from lava. They are the same as those on our own ocean floors!

Venus unmasked! On September 18, 1990, the American probe Magellan scanned the surface of Venus with a radar device and discovered an astonishing site: three large craters, 23 to 31 miles in diameter! Similar to those on the Moon, these are the scars from meteorite impacts. The smallest details visible on this image measure 40 feet across. The probe made another surprising discovery: The volcanoes are still active. Large lava flows and fractures in the crust are evidence of a hot inner fire.

MARS, THE DESERT PLANET

Mars, a red spot in the sky, is not always easy to see from Earth. Yet many legends and fairy tales surround it. The red planet, attributed to the god of war by the Greeks and the Romans, has been famous since the middle of the eighteenth century because of its supposed inhabitants, the Martians. The origin of this Martian myth is easy to trace. Several astronomers observed strange formations on the surface of the planet, which they called "canals." The scientists soon became convinced that these were part of a vast irrigation network, constructed by intelligent beings to supply the desertlike Martian plains with water from the polar caps. They had,

instead, fallen under the spell of a superb optical illusion. The debate among scientists lasted for decades, and the Martian hypothesis was laid to rest only in 1965, when the American probe Mariner 4 flew by Mars. The scientific satellites revealed to an amazed world a planet of vast deserts, enormous extinct volcanoes, and immense dry riverbeds. It is a dead world halfway between the Moon and Antarctica, swept by fantastic

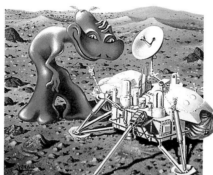

storms that sometimes cover the entire planet with an immense cloud of dust—red, of course.

When the Mariner and Viking space probes first observed Mars, they revealed an austerely beautiful planet. Half the size of Earth, it is nonetheless similar to our planet, with a variety of deserts, volcanoes, ice fields, and wide, dry riverbeds. Volcanic activity, combined with water and wind, has eroded and transformed the planet. Deserts pockmarked with craters cover the southern hemisphere, while enormous volcanoes tower over the north. For a geologist, it is a dream; for life, a nightmare.

A plain of volcanic rocks, boulders, and red sand—this is the site of Utopia Planitia photographed by the Viking probe. Instruments sent to detect life on the planet returned their verdict: negative. The creators of the Viking probe will be able to admire and study this landscape for eight years, analyzing the transformations day by day, season by season. Thousands of images and data concerning the temperatures and the "Mars-quakes" will keep the scientists busy for years.

A dead world, halfway between Antarctica and the Moon

A sunrise over the planet Mars. The morning is still cool, around -94° F, and the clouds in the upper atmosphere form a thin line on the horizon. The Viking probe is flying over the Argyre basin in the southern hemisphere. A large plain, old meteor impact craters, and several mountains lie immobile in the mist.

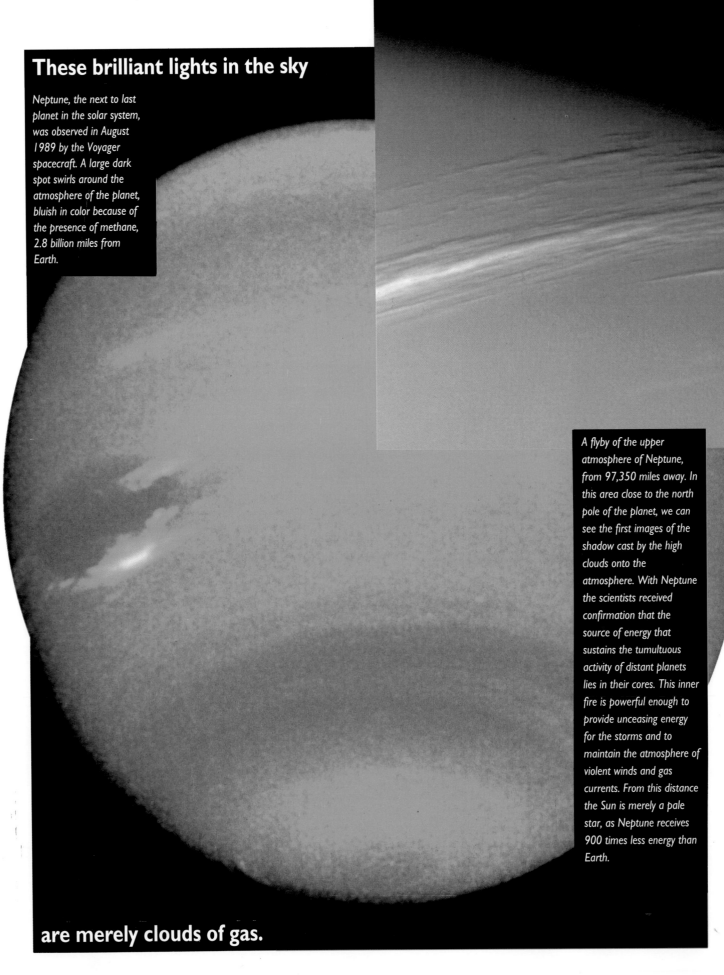

These brilliant lights in the sky

Neptune, the next to last planet in the solar system, was observed in August 1989 by the Voyager spacecraft. A large dark spot swirls around the atmosphere of the planet, bluish in color because of the presence of methane, 2.8 billion miles from Earth.

A flyby of the upper atmosphere of Neptune, from 97,350 miles away. In this area close to the north pole of the planet, we can see the first images of the shadow cast by the high clouds onto the atmosphere. With Neptune the scientists received confirmation that the source of energy that sustains the tumultuous activity of distant planets lies in their cores. This inner fire is powerful enough to provide unceasing energy for the storms and to maintain the atmosphere of violent winds and gas currents. From this distance the Sun is merely a pale star, as Neptune receives 900 times less energy than Earth.

are merely clouds of gas.

THE GIANT PLANETS OF GAS

Extraterrestrial landscapes chart the history of the solar system and raise difficult questions for planetary scientists. One of the them, and it is a major one, concerns Jupiter: What would have happened if Jupiter had been large enough to ignite, like a second Sun?

They are extremely far away and extraordinarily large. They are called Jupiter, Saturn, Uranus, and Neptune and have a common characteristic that is often unknown: they have no surface and consist entirely of gaseous matter! They remained mere points of light in the sky for millennia until 1610 when Galileo aimed his telescope toward the sky. He discovered the reliefs on the Moon, the sunspots, the phases of Venus, the large ball of Jupiter surrounded by four moons, the rings of Saturn, and millions of suns in the Milky Way. Centuries later the Pioneer and Voyager probes sent breathtakingly beautiful photographs back to Earth. Imagine a liquid planet 40 times larger than the Moon: This is Jupiter. A second one, 9 times larger than Earth, so light that it would float on water: Saturn. These were exceptional events in the history of space exploration. At the end of a 12-year voyage, the most famous explorer of modern times was approaching an invisible planet. The complexity of this exploit is similar to sinking a golf ball in a hole 2,170 miles away. This highly successful trip had an additional surprise: None of the world's specialists expected to find a planet as "alive" as this one, so agitated by the atmospheric currents and turbulence that resemble those on Jupiter.

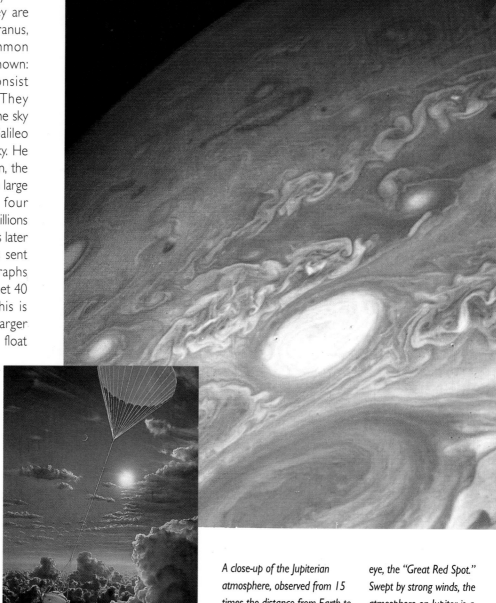

A close-up of the Jupiterian atmosphere, observed from 15 times the distance from Earth to the Moon by the Voyager spacecraft on March 1, 1979. The stormy atmosphere swirls around an enormous cyclopic eye, the "Great Red Spot." Swept by strong winds, the atmosphere on Jupiter is a fascinating, violent, and perpetual whirlwind. Before the end of this century, the Galileo probe should penetrate its center.

RINGS OF ICE

The jewel of the solar system:

A photograph of Saturn taken by the Hubble Space Telescope 860 million miles from Earth. Large, dark structures, evidence of storms that disrupt the atmosphere, are visible on the surface of the gaseous globe.

Saturn—fragile and marvelous!

These are the crowns of the giant planets. Millions of ice particles reflect light from the Sun and shine like snow in the winter Sun. Jupiter, Uranus, and Neptune have them, but the most spectacular and beautiful are those of Saturn, visible even from Earth! In the eyepiece of a good telescope, the rings appear to form a belt around the planet, transforming it into a jewel. For historians of the solar system, these strange formations seem enigmatic. How can we explain the presence of these rings of ice around the giant planets, and how can we analyze their stability and uniform structure? In fact, the ring is formed of many rings; some consist of dark dust specks, others shine brightly white, while some are twisted and others form arcs. Their variety is equaled only by their beauty. It is sometimes claimed that Earth also once had a ring but that it has fallen away. Myth or reality?

Jupiter, Saturn, Uranus, and Neptune have something in common: all are belted with rings of dust, ice, and rock. Yet they are all different. Saturn's rings are wide and numerous, while those of Uranus are thin and recently formed, and Neptune's are fragmented and dispersed. All demonstrate the complexity of the laws that govern the movements and forces in the structure of the solar system, and each tells its own story. It is up to us to learn how to read them.

Right: The nine main rings around Uranus, as observed by Voyager. They are formed from a multitude of fine dust rings that are perfectly aligned around the gaseous globe. These rings are only a few miles wide, and scientists believe they were formed in the recent past. Satellites probably exist in the rings, but they have not yet been discovered.

Below: A close-up of the rings of Saturn, from 6.2 million miles away. This photograph, taken in August 1981 by the Voyager probe, was enhanced with artificial colors to reveal the differences in size between the thousands of small solid bodies that form these rings.

You will never see Saturn like this, unless you are looking through an immense telescope in one of the world's largest observatories on a particularly quiet night. The most astonishing sight, however, aside from the aesthetic element, is the extraordinary thinness of the rings in relation to the planet. If we scaled Saturn down to the size of a steam engine, the rings would be no thicker than a sheet of cigarette paper, or a compact disc only several thousandths of an inch thick!

Planetoids in space

How many planetoids are there? Millions, certainly, perhaps even billions. Famous or unknown, giant or minuscule, all these asteroids—often called planetoids—share the same origin and the same bleak destiny. The planetoids, whether they accompany other planets or wandering stars, do not have an atmosphere, and their surfaces are often severely marked from the major cataclysm of the birth of the solar system. Small spots can be seen on every photograph of the sky taken by a large telescope: These are the thousands of asteroids that cross our sky, approach our globe, bounce off other planets as if they were trampolines, or sleep in an eternal cold, carried along an immutable path. And yet each one, from the smallest speck of planetary dust to the largest of the moons, has a story to tell, one as old as the Sun and the billions of years that have followed its creation. The exploration of these dead worlds will be one of the great challenges for scientists in future centuries.

There are so many that astronomers call them . . .

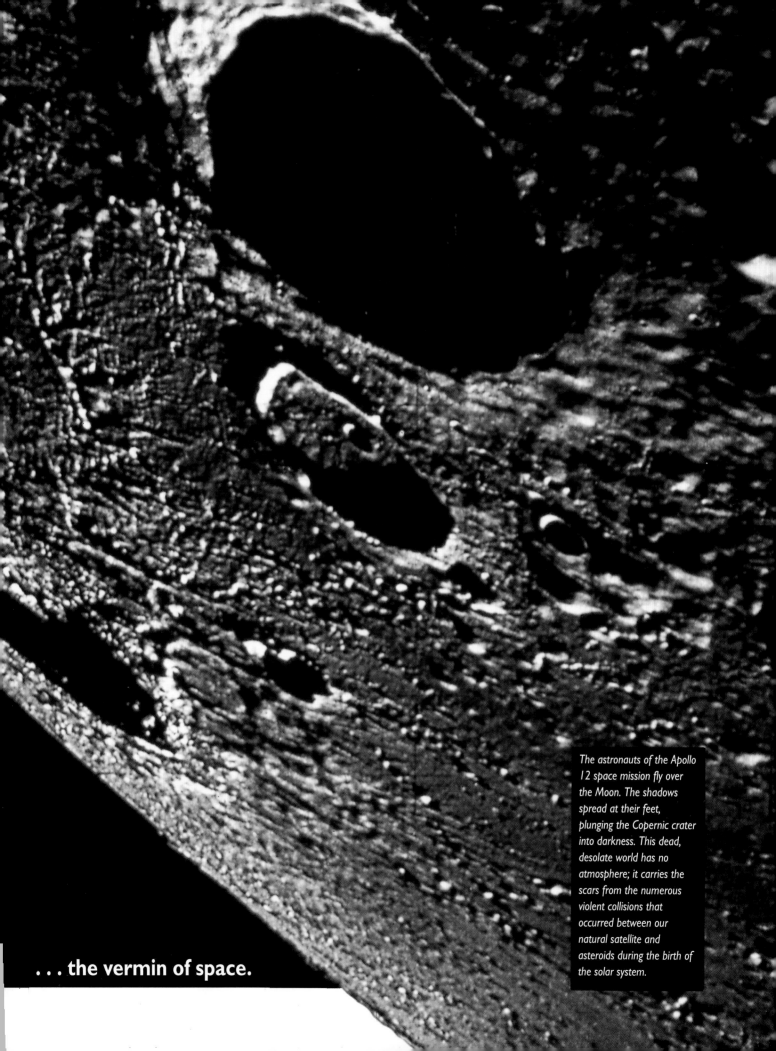

. . . the vermin of space.

The astronauts of the Apollo 12 space mission fly over the Moon. The shadows spread at their feet, plunging the Copernic crater into darkness. This dead, desolate world has no atmosphere; it carries the scars from the numerous violent collisions that occurred between our natural satellite and asteroids during the birth of the solar system.

HALLEY'S COMET—A HEART OF ICE

This comet, with its brilliant tail, returns every 76 years!

Halley's comet, a small, faint, and hazy spot, crosses the Milky Way through the constellation of Scorpio. The date is April 5, 1986, and observatories are monitoring the movements of this majestic comet. The Chinese were the first to sight Halley, in 1057 B.C. For centuries, each of its passages created terror among men. A phenomenon such as this one was considered a certain sign of anger from heaven. The wildest theories were put forth: Some felt it was a burning celestial log meant to stoke the Sun's fire, while others recognized the souls of famous and long-lost people. The astronomers triumphed over these myths, however, by successfully predicting the return of Halley's comet. It will be back on July 29, 2061.

Ready for action, the comet arrives. It appears first as a faint, hazy spot in the sky, imperceptible and as fleecy as a cloud. Night by night, it gets brighter, and soon the famous bright tail of dust and gas is visible. The entire world watches with wonder: Halley has returned! Seventy-six years after its last passage, the famous comet has kept its date. An armada of space probes and thousands of telescopes were on hand to observe and analyze this cosmic event. This is not just any comet! English astronomer Edmond Halley first discovered the periodic nature of this exceptional body. Even though there were a few eccentrics ready to announce the end of the world, this last passage by the comet was, above all, an extraordinary opportunity to confirm the true nature of these rocks of ice. A ring of billions of comets exists within our solar system. From time to time, some split off and hurtle toward the Sun. Heated by the light from the star, these blocks of ice—some of which are one to two miles wide—melt like snow in the spring. The dust particles that escape form shooting stars.

March 13, 1986, was a historic night. Just as the European space probe Giotto was approaching the heart of the comet, an amateur Japanese astronomer photographed Halley from Australia. The brilliant nucleus with a tail and two trails, one formed of gas and the other dust, majestically crosses the starry sky.

This image, re-created by a computer from 60 photographs taken by the Giotto probe, shows the oblong shape of the comet's nucleus, craters, volcanoes of ice, and even a mountainous summit illuminated by the first rays of the Sun. Imagine an enormous avocado or potato 10 miles long, 5 miles wide, and 4.6 miles thick, and you have some idea of the shape of Halley's nucleus.

IN EARTH'S BACKYARD: THE MOON

From Georges Méliès and Tintin to Neil Armstrong,

the Moon has always fascinated people.

This vast, monotonous continent is riddled with craters. Here is the dark side of the Moon as observed by the astronauts on Apollo 11. This invisible side has its own characteristics: a thicker crust, no lava plains, but a multitude of impact craters. It has been the target for most of the meteorite collisions since the beginning of the solar system. This is due to the "leading edge" effect. Just as bugs are smashed on the front windshield of a car rather than on the back, more meteorites crash onto the front side, or leading edge, of the moon. The Moon thus protects us from deadly collisions that could strike Earth.

A trip to the Moon: what an adventure! Everyone has pointed a pair of binoculars or a telescope toward the planet that illuminates our nights. With Saturn, it is the most observed astral body in our near universe. A guided tour of the Moon is a fabulous gift. It offers a multitude of sights: shadows and bright areas, mountains and wide plains, rugged and mild terrain. An excursion to the Moon means a flight over deep craters, precipitous drops into the heart of sinuous canyons, and the discovery of mountains higher than Mont Blanc, jagged with peaks that throw shadows over the dreary, solidified lava plains. It also offers the opportunity to understand the considerable physical influence the Moon exerts on our globe and our activities: tides, eclipses, perhaps even our climate, the reproduction of flora and fauna or artistic inspiration! This companion of the night also has its mysteries. Our understanding of the origin, evolution, structure, and composition of the Moon is still scanty. Neil Armstrong's "small step for man" has been waiting 20 years for the next stage.

An "Earthrise" over the lunar continent, observed by the astronauts on the Apollo 18 mission. The origins of the Earth-Moon system—a unique pair in our solar system—have not been fully explained, although the most accepted hypothesis supports the idea of a collision between Earth and a foreign body; the debris from this event would have formed the Moon.

"Earth is the cradle of humanity, but humanity cannot remain in the cradle forever." The meaning of this maxim by a Soviet pioneer of space exploration became crystal clear for the few men selected to fly over and explore the moon. From 238,057 miles away, our blue planet appears to be fragile and unique. No borders, no countries, just one large body subject to the great laws that govern the universe. The Moon may be dead, but we must protect life on Earth.

A miniature replica of the solar system

Io, Europa, Ganymede, and Callisto are all mythological heroes and heroines. They are also the fascinating satellites of Jupiter, the largest planet in the solar system. In 1610, Galileo first sighted them in his telescope and recorded the presence of these brilliant moons in his journal. They helped Danish astronomer Römer with the first calculations concerning the speed of light, through their hide-and-seek appearances in front of and behind Jupiter. This planetary ballet forms one of the most curious orbital patterns of all the planets. The view from a telescope is fascinating: The moons are visible against a background of Jupiterian storms while their shadows burst forth from behind the planet in a well-ordered line (every six years), sometimes completely eclipsing each other. The Voyager probe offered yet another surprise: This miniature replica of the solar system not only has the same planetary proportions, but is also governed by the same laws and offers, satellite by satellite, a variety and wealth of unsuspected size. These worlds of fire, stone, and ice are the same size as the Moon or Mercury.

The surface of Europa, photographed from 150,000 miles by the Voyager 2 probe in July 1977. It is formed of smooth ice and is scored by a highly complex network of fractures. Only three meteorite impacts have been identified. The maximum temperature on the surface of Europa is 298° F. Scientists who have attempted to reconstruct its history believe that an "ocean" must have covered the satellite after it was formed. It froze quickly, and the surface of this ocean thickened, then fractured under the pressure of sudden movements. This crust of ice is probably not more than 30 to 60 miles deep.

In February 1979, the Voyager 1 probe passed within 78,000 miles of Callisto, the most distant of the Galilean satellites. The numerous bright spots on the dark ice surface are craters from meteorite impacts. At 3.5 billion years, Callisto appears to be the oldest of the satellites.

Astonishing Io appears as an orange-red body, with nuances of yellow, white, and black. For scientists, its extreme volcanic activity can be explained by the combined and opposing gravitational pulls exerted by nearby Jupiter and the three other neighboring satellites. Io is thus constantly expanded and compressed by a gigantic invisible hand that generates intense internal heat and perpetual volcanic eruptions.

WHEN THE SKY FALLS TO EARTH

What can we do with an asteroid or comet that is hurtling toward Earth at more than 62 miles per second? A catastrophe of this magnitude could probably not be predicted, much less avoided. The visible scars on the Moon and on the surface of many satellites are evidence of such an impact: the equivalent of several thousand thermonuclear bombs that would plunge Earth into fire and darkness.

Some 65 million years ago, the masters of the Earth—the dinosaurs—suddenly disappeared. Most theories support the idea of a sudden death that fell from the sky, a collision with an asteroid that plunged Earth into darkness. Deprived of heat and living under a cloud of ash, the giant animals were not able to survive.

In large telescopes they appear as weak as the dimmest stars. Asteroids, dark bodies with diameters measuring from a few yards up to 60 miles across, are the most primitive mini-planets in the solar system. Shortly after the birth of our Sun, the planets were formed from a vast cloud of dust and gas, which through successive collisions collected into planetary masses. The particles that escaped the great cataclysms of this period did not become part of a single planet. Thousands of these particles form the famous "asteroid belt," which lies in an unstable orbit between Mars and Jupiter. Others wander through space, colliding with previously formed planets and satellites. Although these events happened in the past, the danger of a collision from an asteroid striking Earth cannot be excluded. Worse—it is inevitable! Close to 100 asteroids, measuring 328 feet to 3.1 miles in diameter, could cross Earth's orbit. Craters from meteorite strikes exist on the surface of Earth, and scientists sometimes associate these events with the massive disappearance of animal species. Even though it has not been proven that the great dinosaurs were a victim of such a disaster, it is certain that a major cosmic collision would plunge mankind into the worst imaginable nightmare.

One thousand times more powerful than the Hiroshima bomb! The power of the heat and shock wave that sterilized this entire region of Arizona for over 3,860 square miles was estimated by scientists at 15 megatons. The most extraordinary fact is that this cataclysm was caused by a meteorite no larger than several dozen yards in diameter, called "Canyon Diablo." The odds of a catastrophic collision taking place in the next 50 years has been estimated by NASA as 1 in 6,000—an unsettling probability, to be sure.

Phobos, one of the two satellites of Mars, is an asteroid. Photographed from 372.6 miles away by the Viking probe, its surface conditions reveal the violence of the impact that formed its main crater, Stickney. Fractures opened up during the collision, but this satellite, some 12.4 miles in diameter, withstood the impact.

An unknown trail moves rapidly across the photographic plate of a monitoring telescope. Toutatis was caught in the nets set by astronomers to catch asteroids wandering in the solar system. There are dozens of thousands of these celestial bodies in our skies.

An Earth/asteroid collision? . . . Inevitable!

Crater Mound, near Flagstaff in Arizona, measures 3,960 feet in diameter and is 660 feet deep. Approximately 25,000 years ago, an iron meteorite, 82.5 feet across, struck the planet at a speed of 62,100 miles per hour . . . with catastrophic results.

STONES FROM THE SKY

A cut of an iron meteorite carefully preserved in a Tucson laboratory. These meteorites are ancient and have been torn from a larger body: a planet or asteroid.

This is "Orgeuil 235," a tiny piece of the famous meteorite, a few pounds in weight, that struck Orgeuil, near Montauban (France), during the night of May 14, 1864. An analysis of its composition allowed scientists to draw up an initial list of cosmic elements. It represents an "astronomical" Rosetta stone.

A trail of fire slashes across the sky. Noiselessly, it illuminates the landscape for an instant with a faint light, then disappears as quickly as it came. The shooting star left behind nothing more than a fleeting trace that vanished rapidly. This is not a sun falling from the sky; it is, instead, a speck of cosmic dust disintegrating in Earth's upper atmosphere. There is nothing mysterious in the origins of these shooting stars. Earth regularly passes through clouds of dust. These particles, left behind by comets, produce spectacular showers of meteorites. The most famous shower, the Perseid, is at its brightest around August 12, with a minimum of 50 meteorites per hour in the sky. It is a free display visible with the naked eye for anyone willing to leave behind the lights of the cities and readjust to the dark night sky. These meteorites are mere specks of dust; some rare ones, however, reach Earth. Every year our planet receives some 200,000 meteorites, which represent approximately 10,000 tons of cosmic matter. This is a veritable treasure for archaeologists of the solar system, who often find incredible surprises. Some meteorites have been identified as originating on the Moon and even on Mars!

Scientific research of stones from the sky, made popular by Hergé with his famous *Mysterious Star* expedition, is not an easy undertaking. An estimated 500 meteorites, weighing anything from a few grains to several hundred pounds, strike Earth every year. The trouble is finding them. The icy desert of Antarctica has proven to be an ideal site for meteorite hunters. Protected by the glacial ice, easily identifiable and "unpolluted," meteorites await, ready to reveal their secrets to probing scientists.

Trails of fire in the sky . . .

During time-lapse photographs of the sky, Earth rotates and the stars form great arcs; the farther away they are from Polaris (the star that indicates due north in the Northern Hemisphere), the greater the arc. This harmonious movement is disrupted by trails of fire that burn across the starry sky; these are shooting stars.

. . . shooting stars

True showers of falling stars are rare, and most are unpredictable. But when Earth moves through a cloud of particularly dense dust particles, thousands of meteorites per hour disintegrate in the upper atmosphere.

Suns of the cosmos

Our Sun is not alone is the sky: small, large, dwarf, giant, red, yellow, and blue suns all exist. Their variety and wealth have been revealed during explorations. Astronomers in large observatories have given up trying to count the number of stars visible on the photographic plates and now find it easier to simply accept that there are an infinite number. Our human references are no longer valid in the language of the stars. If you could observe, unaided, the star closest to Earth, then use a good pair of binoculars, a telescope, and finally the largest telescope in the world, you would see that it does not change in size—it is too far away to reveal the smallest detail. At a speed of 186,000 miles per second it would take an interstellar voyager four years and three months to reach it! The cosmos teaches us that the universe has a history, that stars—just like human beings—are born, live, and die, sometimes in an overwhelming cataclysm. And above all, on the roof of our planet-observatory, we, as attentive and amazed spectators, can watch the life of the cosmos. And what a fascinating one it is!

One of the regions of the sky that contains the densest concentration of stars is obviously the Milky Way. Entire clouds of suns seem to be bound together in the area around the Sagittarius constellation. This is an illusion because the distances separating these suns are, quite simply, astronomical.

A DIP IN THE MILKY WAY

We have lost touch with the sky in our everyday lives. The reason is simple: electricity has become the archenemy of astronomy. This artificial day created by urban lighting leaves little room for the nocturnal landscape. Worse, in the large cities it blocks it totally by reflecting back the dust and gas that covers most urban centers. The sky is threatened, and "light" pollution has forced many observatories to flee to the atmospheric calm of mountaintops.

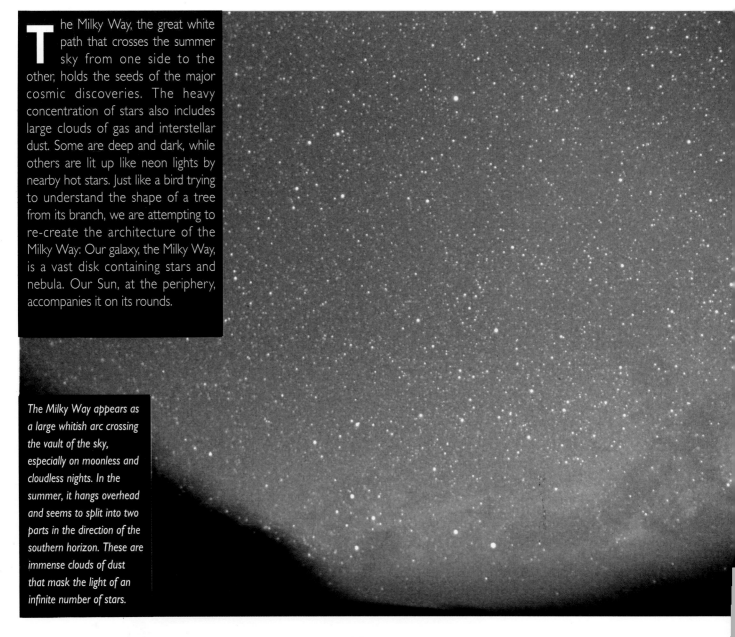

The Milky Way, the great white path that crosses the summer sky from one side to the other, holds the seeds of the major cosmic discoveries. The heavy concentration of stars also includes large clouds of gas and interstellar dust. Some are deep and dark, while others are lit up like neon lights by nearby hot stars. Just like a bird trying to understand the shape of a tree from its branch, we are attempting to re-create the architecture of the Milky Way. Our galaxy, the Milky Way, is a vast disk containing stars and nebula. Our Sun, at the periphery, accompanies it on its rounds.

The Milky Way appears as a large whitish arc crossing the vault of the sky, especially on moonless and cloudless nights. In the summer, it hangs overhead and seems to split into two parts in the direction of the southern horizon. These are immense clouds of dust that mask the light of an infinite number of stars.

A close-up of the edge of the Milky Way. In this region of the constellation of Sagittarius, toward the center of our galaxy, a high density of stars borders gaseous nebula, large clouds of dark dust and small globular clusters, while shooting stars make brief appearances.

Here are two marvels of the summer sky in the Milky Way: the nebulas of Lagoon and Trifid, visible to the naked eye and spectacular with a pair of binoculars. The stars, gas, and clouds of dust appear to be compressed, but in fact a nebula such as the large red Trifid lies some 3,000 light-years from earth, measures 15 light-years across, and contains a mass equivalent to 150 stars like the Sun!

NEBULAS: CLOUDS OF STARDUST

No evolution takes place in the universe without a catastrophe. When a star is born, the temperatures become extreme, and powerful winds sweep away everything in their wake. Earth itself would be no more than a straw blown in the wind. The stars pay for this violence with their lives: too large, they survive only a few million years; too small, they are "devoured" by companion stars in immense cataclysms. Billions of years later, calm returns once again after these terrible births.

One of the greatest challenges of modern astrophysics was to understand how, and to see where, stars are formed. The birth of a star was observed, accidentally, in 1936. One night a star named FU Orionis was born in the great nebula of Orion. Massive amounts of matter were condensing at this spot, due to compression and shock waves. Studies indicated that these bodies of interstellar matter were collapsing in on themselves under the effect of gravity. In less than a million years a nucleus had formed in the center of the condensation, dense and hot enough to emit its own radiation. A star was born! And astronomers had discovered its cradle in the heart of the nebula. This area contained a sufficient quantity of gases to produce new stars, and the ignition of these new bodies generated the shock waves required to form new stellar embryos. In these enormous cocoons of gas, we can observe the simultaneous birth of systems containing dozens of stars. Young and hot, they leave behind their nebulous origins and release their first nuclear emissions that will shine for billions of years.

A star is born!

Approximately two million years ago, the Cone Nebula gave birth to a group of extremely hot blue stars. The creation of these stars, 2,000 light-years from Earth, generated a galactic tidal wave that struck the surrounding stellar regions. The stellar winds ripping through the nebula created what looks like enormous torn sails.

BILLIONS OF SUNS

The universe of the suns is a reflection of our own human-scaled world, at first view, composed of similar members but in reality all different.

When the designers of the Pioneer probe wanted to place an image of a man and a woman on a plate attached to the side of the probe as a welcome to any signs of extraterrestrial intelligence, they confronted a fundamental problem: how to find a single image that would represent humanity in all of its wealth and diversity. If, by chance, an intergalactic vessel intercepts our small probe lost in the stars, its voyagers will discover a man with fuzzy hair, almond-shaped eyes, and white skin! Similarly in the universe there are bodies of all sizes, colors, and temperatures. Some live in pairs, some in families composed of three of four members; others, like our Sun, are solitary. From dwarfs to supergiants, the stars have been classified by astronomers according to two criteria: temperature and brightness. Yet this identification applies only to the most famous stars. Other small stars such as our own—precious sources of heat for life—are undoubtedly hidden in the anonymous mass.

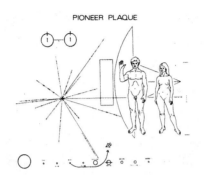

PIONEER PLAQUE

The most massive stars will live for only a few million years. These stars represent the minority, however, since astronomers estimate that 75% of the stars have a mass equal to or smaller than the Sun's. Sirius has a companion star that is smaller than Earth. Among the famous giants, Capella (in the constellation of Auriga) holds the current record with a diameter estimated to be 2,700 times larger than the Sun's. If this supergiant occupied the place of our Sun, it would swallow up all the planets as far as Saturn.

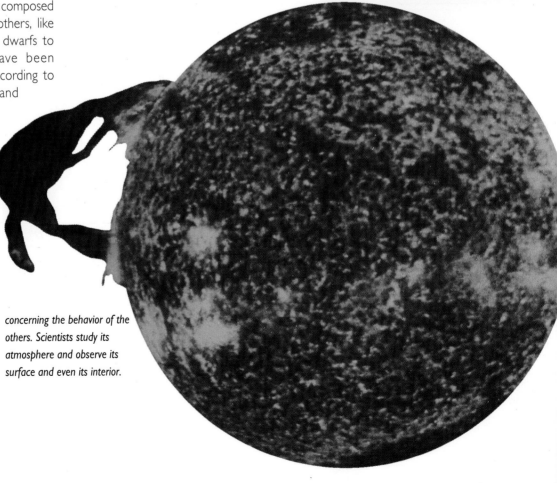

This star is five billion years old. Four million tons of matter are converted into energy and released every second. Huge storms sometimes shoot out brilliant and terrible trails of fire. This is the Sun, the only star whose surface we can observe. Our Sun is the best source of information concerning the behavior of the others. Scientists study its atmosphere and observe its surface and even its interior.

A beacon in the dark! This giant yellow star shines brightly in the famous constellation of Orion. Emerging from clouds of gas and dust, it is shadowed by one of the mythical figures of astronomy: the dark Horsehead Nebula.

STELLAR ALCHEMY

Stars do not have an eternal life. Just like human beings, they are born, live, and die, returning to space most of the matter from which they were created. The type of death depends on the mass of the star. The small ones endure a long and spectacular agony and form "smoke rings" around themselves, called planetary nebulas. During the last moments of celestial life, as observed in the large telescopes, the star expels a ring of matter, enriched with new chemical elements, which will be pulled together to form new stars. As if attacked by spasms and violent convulsions, it ejects its external layers to a distance several light-months away. These contractions raise the temperature of the star, which illuminates its own death throes. The sight of a dying star is similar to a sunset: grandiose and solemn. Little by little, the waves of ejected matter slow down and stop. In the center lies a bare stellar nucleus, not much larger than our Moon, that is slowly and surely extinguished.

◄ A star in a bubble! This is a totally unknown star, N 47 + 4, a planetary nebula that is virtually invisible, even to the large telescopes, revealed here through the powerful techniques of image processing. In the center reigns a white dwarf, the last stage in the life of a small star as it burns up its final reserves of gas.

Helix, less than 600 light-years from Earth, is the closest known planetary nebula. It is approximately 4 light-years in diameter, and in the center lies an extremely hot white dwarf. The reasons for its curious shape have not yet been explained. ►

We are formed from elements that all come from space.

At their death, stars disperse their matter into space. These colored trails spreading over billions of miles are the debris of a dying star. Atoms meet and form molecules and dust particles in these shreds of matter. The astrophysicists are certain that the planets of the solar system were created from this dust, and from these molecules were formed plants, animals, and man. The origins of life and the elements that comprise it must therefore be sought in the sky.

SUPERNOVAS

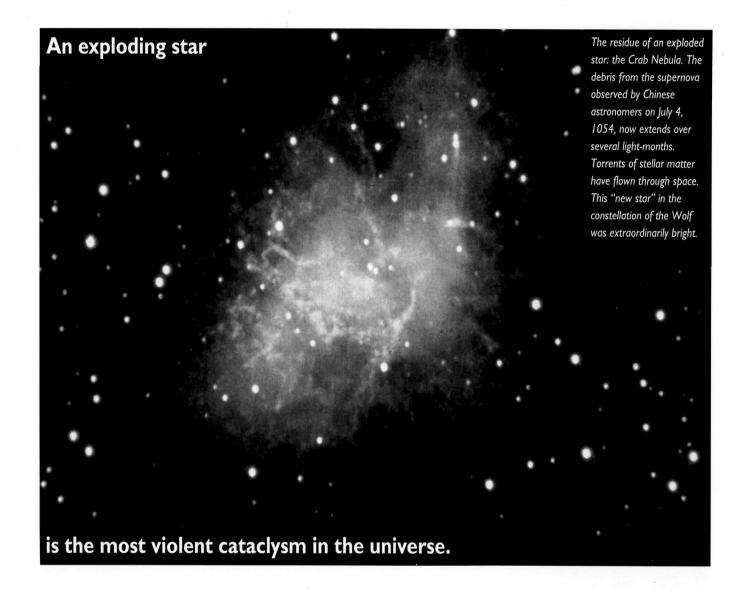

An exploding star

is the most violent cataclysm in the universe.

The residue of an exploded star: the Crab Nebula. The debris from the supernova observed by Chinese astronomers on July 4, 1054, now extends over several light-months. Torrents of stellar matter have flown through space. This "new star" in the constellation of the Wolf was extraordinarily bright.

During the night of February 23, 1987, Canadian astronomer Ian Shelton, who was working at Las Campanas observatory in Chile, left the white dome of the building to walk under the star-filled sky. The evening was warm, and by habit he looked up at the familiar white spot. The Large Magellanic Cloud was a commonplace sight for a professional observer: this faint galaxy, companion of our Milky Way, looks like a nebulous, cloudy patch to the naked eye. But Shelton detected a light in the middle of the cloud—a new light that had not been there the previous night. A star had just exploded, creating a supernova. The violence of the explosion was beyond calculation. In one month, the star released as much energy as does our Sun in 10 billion years. Observatories around the world, notified immediately, aimed their telescopes at this cosmic catastrophe, and scientific satellites were redirected to capture this new target. The event made headlines, and with reason: A supernova is a rare event. Not since 1604, when Kepler observed a supernova, had the death of such a close star been observed. This giant star, 700,000 light-years from Earth, collapsed on itself, and then like a spring that has been wound too tight, expelled its entire atmosphere in a gigantic cataclysm. Astronomers observing the residue of the explosion hoped to find a pulsar or a possible black hole, but were disappointed. They have not yet been detected, and the quest for the mysterious object, the black hole, remains as elusive as ever.

The brightest star in the center of this image, above the Tarantula Nebula, is the supernova in the Large Magellanic Cloud. It appeared for the first time during the night of February 23, 1987, visible to the unaided eye. Some 170,000 years ago, a blue giant exploded, and the shock wave is just hitting Earth now. At 270 billion °F, this hellish light is the hottest place in the universe.

Far away in space, far away in time

Less than 100 years ago we didn't know that the Sun and all the stars that surround us belong to the same family. We had no idea that it was such a large one, consisting of billions of members, themselves formed of hundreds of millions of stars. It is a dizzying prospect. It was not easy to calculate the distances that separate us from these island universes and to reconstruct their histories. Unsolved enigmas linger on still. The discovery of the universe led us to recognize that it has not always existed. This theory, called the "big bang," postulates an expanding universe, in which all the galaxies are moving away from one another—an infinite universe that extends everywhere and in all directions simultaneously! By looking far off in space, astronomers have also gone back in time. The light messages from galaxies billions of light-years away are also billions of years old and reveal the cosmos at its most primitive time in history.

The fabulous galaxy of Sombrero, 44 million light-years from Earth, would be a serious contestant in a galactic beauty contest. Three billion stars are contained in this bulb-shaped body, which is divided by a dark band. Dark clouds absorb the light behind it. This is an entire "universe" outside our own galaxy!

Infinite universes

THE MILKY WAY, AN ISLAND IN SPACE

Leaving the region of the Sun is to venture into space and space times that defy the imagination. It is necessary to determine specific locations and to evaluate the distances that separate us from other cosmic bodies. For generations of astronomers, the bright points in the sky merely formed a two-dimensional painting, without relief. Before astronomers discovered a method for distinguishing distant objects from close ones, large ones from small, the structure of the sky was extremely mysterious. Herschel, observing the nebula, was the first to suspect that to an observer located sufficiently far away, the Milky Way would also look like a nebula. Gradually the existence of several galaxies was confirmed. Even better, astronomers were able to prove that the Sun and all its counterparts in the Milky Way belong to a common structure that forms an enormous family of 100 billion stars. This is the galaxy, our galaxy. It has the shape of a compact disc revolving around a central core. On one of its spiral arms, 27,000 light-years from the center, our Sun moves, completing a revolution every 250 million years!

Our vision of the universe has been altered dramatically with the discovery of other galaxies. The Milky Way, for example, is so vast that if we scaled it down to the size of Europe, the Earth—smaller than an atom of dust—would barely be visible in an electronic microscope. Comprehending an immensity of this nature is not an easy task.

Our closest neighbor, the Andromeda Galaxy. It appears to the naked eye as a vast nebulous patch and is 2 million light-years from Earth. A nucleus of old stars in the center dominates brilliantly, while spiral arms on the outside are inhabited by new stars. Surrounded by two satellite galaxies, it completes a revolution every 200 million years. The light reaching us today left Andromeda when man first began to appear on Earth.

Celestial wheels revolving in a vacuum

The galaxy, the Milky Way, as seen from "outside." This image of the structure of our galaxy was created by combining several photographs of the sky made by the COBE satellite. It confirms that the Milky Way is shaped like a flattened disk, swollen in the center, and 100,000 light-years in diameter.

This superb spiral galaxy is in the constellation of Ursa Major (the Great Bear). At "only" 15 million light-years from Earth, the Messier 101 Galaxy is, in shape, a sister to our Milky Way. It has a central core, spinning spiral arms, and hundreds of billions of stars just like our Sun.

IN THE HEART OF GLOBULAR CLUSTERS

The globular clusters are all extremely old, evidence of the first stages in the creation of the galaxies. As vestiges from an era when stars could still be formed outside of the disk of the Milky Way, they are also actual cocoons. Paradoxically, these sparkling jewels are now sterile, since they exhausted their reserves of gas long ago. These gases provide the matter from which new stars can be born. With the space telescope, astronomers will be able to pierce the core of these ancestors. Will they find there the secret of the clusters' longevity?

They exist in a large spherical halo around galaxies, contain from 100,000 to several million stars, and fascinate observers with their extraordinarily compact shapes. The globular clusters are hunted almost everywhere in the universe by astronomers because they provide precious information about the dynamics and evolution of the galaxies. These large swarms in space are some of the oldest inhabitants of the galaxies. They are often more than 10 billion years old and, as such, are the oldest evidence of the galactic genesis. Thus the "primitive soup," from which the stars in the center and in the arms of galaxies were formed, has its "lumps." They are bodies that are separate from the others, true fossils from a time that no longer exists. In the center of this wreath of stars lies a menacing and titanic mass, a fleecy cloud cut through with dark bands, where more than 100 billion suns shine in unison: this spiral galaxy, seen from below, is our own Milky Way!

Astronomers have placed their hopes on the Hubble Space Telescope, placed in orbit around the Earth by the space shuttle to observe the universe. What it will see depends on its precision; a faulty mirror is preventing optimal use of the telescope.

Authentic fossils lost in the mists of time

The globular cluster of Toucan 47, 13,000 light-years from Earth, contains more than a million stars. This is one of the youngest clusters in the galaxy—a mere 10 billion years old. It appears as a fuzzy star to the unaided eye, but in a telescope Toucan 47, near the Large Magellanic Cloud, is a spectacular sight.

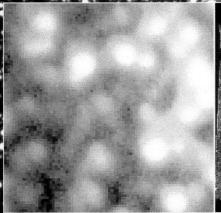 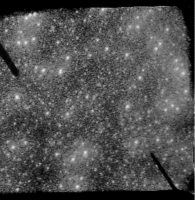

These two somewhat esoteric images represent a major inroad into invisible worlds. To the left, the center of a globular cluster observed from a telescope on Earth: cloudy, fuzzy spots. To the right, the same image photographed by the Hubble Space Telescope. Clear and precise, these stars lie in the center of a globular cluster.

THE OCEAN OF GALAXIES

"Name any figure—as large as you like," say mathematicians, "infinity is larger still." This bewilderment in the face of the unknown seizes us whenever we try to represent the universe. Planets around a star, a star among a hundred billion others in the galaxy, and billions of billions of galaxies: this is the unsettling and fascinating landscape of an infinite universe. However far we look, in space and in time, the universe is uniformly populated with galaxies. Our own Milky Way forms a group—a cluster—with some twenty other galaxies. This "Local Group," as it is called by astronomers, is itself part of a larger group: the Local Supercluster of Virgo that consists of thousands of galaxies. This organization is multiplied literally endlessly. The superclusters are to the galaxies what the Milky Way is to the stars: a family with its rules, its fundamental forces, and a history that goes back to the creation of matter. Yet the exploration of the major structures of the universe has only just begun; the cosmos hides its secrets well!

The Sun belongs to the Milky Way, just as our galaxy belongs to the supercluster of Virgo. This supercluster—several elements of which we see here—consists of several thousands of galaxies distributed in a volume measuring some 50 million light-years in diameter. The blurred white spots are thousands of billions of suns.

These two galaxies were not born as twins. According to astronomers, they are in "interaction"; in other words, they intersect and bounce off each other at speeds of a few hundred miles per second. During these collisions, none of the billions of stars in the galaxies touch one another. The masses of gas in the two spiral galaxies do, however, interpenetrate one another. Dragged along in their wake, they throw out bridges of stars that sweep out into the vastness of space.

How was the universe created and how will it evolve?

The universe is uniformly populated with a host of galaxies

Two galaxies, hand in hand. The famous double galaxy of the Hunting Dogs (or Canes Venatici), 35 million light-years from Earth, is a typical example of the type of twins united by bridges of matter. Stars, gas, and nebulas form these arms that are linked together by the pull of gravity.

THE INVISIBLE UNIVERSE

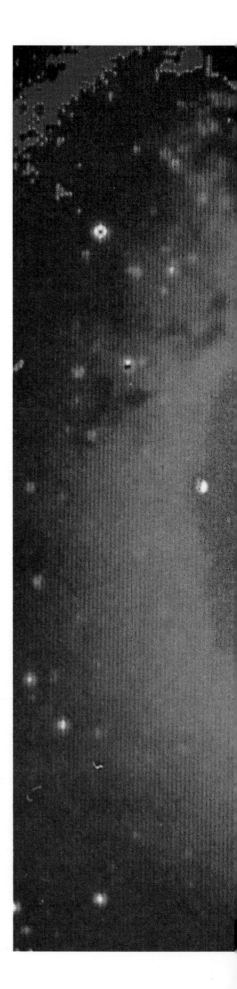

False colors and image processing form this photograph of the large and mysterious radio galaxy of Alpha Centauri. At 10 million light-years from Earth, it is one of the closest known active galaxies. Powerful radio emissions, proof of tremendously violent phenomena, escape from its nucleus. Specialists suspect that this galaxy may be hiding a black hole.

We revolve around a yellow star, the Sun. Our eye is naturally adjusted to this section of the light scale that we call the "visible." We see as red a 932° F fire; yellow, the Sun with a surface temperature of around 10,832° F; blue, a giant star burning at 36,032° F.

But these colors do not include the complete range of radiation. For example, when we lie on the beach at noon on a hot day in August, other electromagnetic rays reach us: heat is infrared radiation, while sunburn is caused by ultraviolet rays. From the strongest to the weakest, from gamma, X, and ultraviolet radiation to visible, infrared, and radio rays, the "electromagnetic spectrum" from the stars and galaxies reveal the conditions under which they exist.

This astronomy of the invisible attempts to hunt down the most extreme conditions in the universe. Extremely cold molecular clouds have been found, even though they are not illuminated by hot stars, and powerful nuclear emissions have been recorded by special telescopes. They enable astronomers to explore the exotic pulsars, quasars, and black holes.

The exploration of the universe today begins with our own environment and extends to include the solar system, our stellar surroundings within a radius of a few hundred light-years, the galaxy, its neighbors, and, finally, as far as we can see, to quasars more than 10 billion light-years away. This exploration is confronting tremendous problems: after a certain distance, it is very complicated to take reliable measurements since only the brightest objects remain visible. A representation of the "universe in its entirety" depends on the precision of the calculations and on the number of objects observed.

There is no doubt—our vision of the universe is certain to change!

The use of new techniques to process images from the cosmos has considerably transformed our vision of the world. The "old" universe now appears as the visible part of an immensely larger, richer, and even more surprising cosmos. By dissecting the light from galaxies, astronomers have obtained precious information. Matter in all its states—tremendously hot, cold, violent, or inert—has now been identified and has provided a more complete, and more complex, understanding of space.

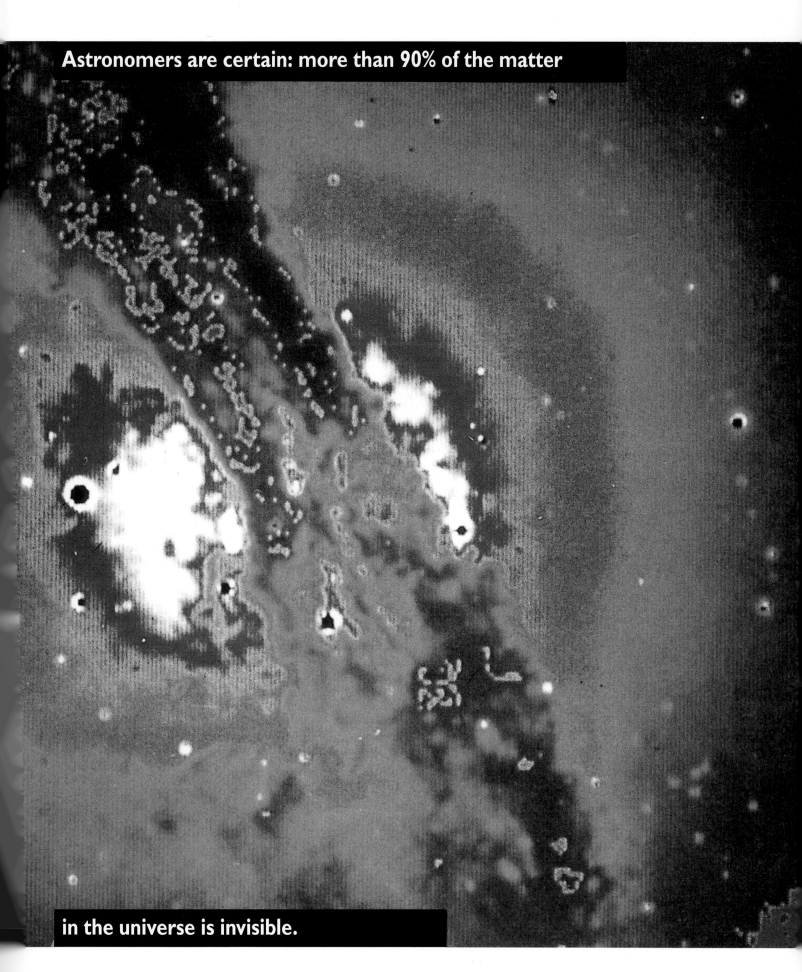

Astronomers are certain: more than 90% of the matter

in the universe is invisible.

PHOTO CREDITS

P 2-3: © S. Brunier/Ciel et Espace; P 2: left, © S. Brunier/Ciel et Espace; right, © S. Brunier/Ciel et Espace; P 3: © S. Brunier/Ciel et Espace. P 4: top, © J. F. Leoni/Ciel et Espace; bottom, © Lick/Ciel et Espace. P 5: © VSGS/Ciel et Espace. P 6: © NASA/Ciel et Espace. P 7: top, © Ciel et Espace; bottom, © NASA/Ciel et Espace. P 8: top, © D. Hardy/Picto; bottom, © NASA/Ciel et Espace. P 9: © NASA/Ciel et Espace. P 10: right, © NASA/Ciel et Espace; left, © NASA/Ciel et Espace. P 11: top © NASA/Ciel et Espace; bottom, © L. Bret/Ciel et Espace. P 12: © NASA/Ciel et Espace. P 13: top, © NASA/Ciel et Espace; bottom left, © NASA/Ciel et Espace; bottom right, © NASA/Ciel et Espace. P 14: © Antoine de Saint-Exupéry/Le Petit prince; éditions Galimmard, 1951. P 14-15: © NASA/Ciel et Espace. P 16: top, © G. Dagli Orti; middle, © ESA/Ciel et Espace; bottom, © J.-L. Charmet. P 17: Cosmos/J. Baum/Science Photo Library; right, © ESA/Ciel et Espace. P 18: left, © Lapi-Viollet; right © NASA/Ciel et Espace. P 19: © NASA/Ciel et Espace. P 20: top left, © NASA/Ciel et Espace; top right, © Edimedia/P. Hinous; bottom, © NASA/Ciel et Espace. P 21: © NASA/Ciel et Espace. P 22: © Jacana/ F. Gohier. P 23: top © SIC/Ciel et Espace; middle, © Toutatis/Ciel et Espace; bottom, © A. Cirou/Ciel et Espace. P 24: top left, © SIC/Ciel et Espace; bottom, © Hergé Casterman; top right, © Alain Suberbic/Ciel et Espace. P 25: © SIC/Ciel et Espace. P 26-27: © ROE/Ciel et Espace; p 27: © Hamel/Ciel et Espace; P 28-29: © S. Brunien; p 29: © ESO/Ciel et Espace; bottom, © Ciel et Espace. P 30: bottom, © S. Brunier/Ciel et Espace; top, © A. Fujii/Ciel et Espace; P 31: © AAT/Ciel et Espace. P 32: top, © NASA/Ciel et Espace; bottom, © NOAO/Ciel et Espace. P 33: © AFA; P 34: top, © Caltsoh/Ciel et Espace; middle © ESO/Ciel et Espace; bottom, © Hachette; P 35: © CFH/Ciel et Espace. P 36: © NOAO/Ciel et Espace. P 37: © ESO/Ciel et Espace. P 38-39: © ESO/Ciel et Espace. P 40: © HALE/Ciel et Espace. P 41: © CFH/Ciel et Espace; bottom, © NASA/Ciel et Espace. P 42: © NASA/Ciel et Espace. P 43: © ESO/Ciel et Espace, bottom, © NASA/Ciel et Espace. P 44: © NOAO/Ciel et Espace. P 45: © CFHT/Ciel et Espace. P 46-47: © NOAO/Ciel et Espace.
Front Cover: Insert © S. Brunier/Ciel et Espace; background © NASA/Ciel et Espace. Back Cover: © S. Brunier/Ciel et Espace

Design and Layout: Etienne Hénocq - François Huertas.

Copyright © 1992 by Hachette-Paris
Translation copyright © 1993 by New Discovery Books

New Discovery Books
Macmillan Publishing Company
866 Third Avenue
New York, NY 10022

Maxwell Macmillan Canada, Inc.
1200 Eglinton Avenue East
Suite 200
Don Mills, Ontario M3C 3N1

Macmillan Publishing Company is part of the Maxwell Communication Group of Companies.

First Edition

Printed in the United States of America

10 9 8 7 6 5 4 3 2 1

ISBN 0-02-781650-4
Library of Congress Catalog Card Number 93-20078